COOL DADDY RAT

Kristyn Crow   illustrated by **Mike Lester**

G. P. Putnam's Sons

Cool Daddy Rat
shooby dooby doo dat
grabbed his hat in his rat flat
zowie zowie zoo zat

and said good-bye to his spry guy.

huggy wuggy boo bat

"I'll see ya, Ace. Gotta scat and play my bass."

And so he . . .

ZOW!

rode a train 'neath
the rain drains

click
clickety
rat tat

got to scat for a fat cat

witty kitty shoo bat

went an odd way

down Broadway

hippy zippy
zee zat

and found Ace in his bass case!

peeky squeaky who dat

TAP
TAP
TAP

"Real sneaky, son. Now tell Mama what you've done."

And then he . . .

caught a gig at the Big Swig
hello fellows **pat pat**

plucked the blues on a shmooze cruise
shmoozy doozy chit chat

made a mime stare
in Times Square

lookie
lookie
see
dat

and filled the street
with his sweet beat.

"Daddy's such a cool rat!"

"You like my jazz?
It's the best this city has."

And then he . . .

strummed a solo in SoHo

jazzy spazzy zee zat

played nonstop on a rooftop

yipsy tipsy top dat

and heard the noise of his boy's voice.

He bowed proud to a wowed crowd!

"I didn't know you could scat!

We'd better scurry, your mama's gonna worry."

And so they . . .

hailed a cab to their rad pad

hurry scurry rat tat

kept their sights on those night lights

shooby dooby doo dat

fell asleep to beep, beep, beep, beep

ZZZZZZZZZZZZZZZZZZZZZZZZZZZZZZZZZZZZzzzzzz

Cool Daddy Rat.

peeky squeaky who dat

For my real cool daddy, Robert Williams Riley.—K. C.

To Roy and Condi, who love rats, birds and naps.—M. L.

G. P. PUTNAM'S SONS
A division of Penguin Young Readers Group.
Published by The Penguin Group.
Penguin Group (USA) Inc., 375 Hudson Street, New York, NY 10014, U.S.A.
Penguin Group (Canada), 90 Eglinton Avenue East, Suite 700, Toronto, Ontario M4P 2Y3, Canada (a division of Pearson Penguin Canada Inc.).
Penguin Books Ltd, 80 Strand, London WC2R 0RL, England.
Penguin Ireland, 25 St. Stephen's Green, Dublin 2, Ireland (a division of Penguin Books Ltd.).
Penguin Group (Australia), 250 Camberwell Road, Camberwell, Victoria 3124, Australia (a division of Pearson Australia Group Pty Ltd).
Penguin Books India Pvt Ltd, 11 Community Centre, Panchsheel Park, New Delhi – 110 017, India.
Penguin Group (NZ), 67 Apollo Drive, Rosedale, North Shore 0745, Auckland, New Zealand (a division of Pearson New Zealand Ltd.).
Penguin Books (South Africa) (Pty) Ltd, 24 Sturdee Avenue, Rosebank, Johannesburg 2196, South Africa.
Penguin Books Ltd, Registered Offices: 80 Strand, London WC2R 0RL, England.

Text copyright © 2008 by Kristyn Crow. Illustrations copyright © 2008 by Mike Lester.

Library of Congress Cataloging-in-Publication Data
Crow, Kristyn. Cool Daddy Rat / Kristyn Crow ; illustrated by Mike Lester. p. cm. Summary: A young rat hides in his father's bass case and tags along as he plays and scats around the big city.
[1. Jazz—Fiction. 2. Musicians—Fiction. 3. Rats—Fiction. 4. New York (N.Y.)—Fiction. 5. Stories in rhyme.] I. Lester, Mike, ill. II. Title. PZ8.3.C8858Coo 2008 [E]—dc22 2006020533

ISBN 978-0-399-24375-2
1 3 5 7 9 10 8 6 4 2